Ann—my editor and friend, for your trust and honesty
Martha and Basho—my rocks
Abi, Luka, Ryan, and Harper—the wonder in my life
Emily Brontë—the black widow spider who so inspired

www.hmhco.com

The text of this book is set in Oldbook ITC.
The illustrations are mixed media paintings.
Library of Congress Cataloging-in-Publication Data is on file.
ISBN 978-0-544-41686-4

Manufactured in USA
PHX 10 9 8 7 6 5 4 3
4500568041

In happy hours, when the imagination
Wakes like a wind at midnight, and the soul
Trembles in all its leaves, it is a joy
To be uplifted on its wings, and listen
To the prophetic voices in the air
That call us onward.
—Longfellow

THE WHISPER

PAMELA ZAGARENSKI

Houghton Mifflin Harcourt
Boston   New York

There once was
a little girl who loved stories.
She loved how the words and pictures
took her to new and secret places
that existed in a world all her own.
The characters became her friends,
and quite often she grew to love them.

One afternoon while
waiting for school to be dismissed,
the little girl noticed a mysterious book
perched high up on a single shelf.

"What's that book?"
she asked her teacher.

"That is a magical book of stories,"
replied her teacher.
"It was a gift from my grandmother
when I was just about your age.
I have an idea.
Would you like to borrow it
for the night?"

"Oh yes, please! Thank you!"
said the little girl,
just as the clock struck three.

The teacher gave her the book,
and with great anticipation,
the little girl sprinted out the door
and ran all the way home.

Once home, the little girl greeted her dog and ate supper, and when she was just about to burst with excitement, she escaped to her room to read.

The little girl opened the book and began turning through the pages one by one. Each picture was more beautiful and curious than the next. By the time she arrived at the very last page, she could scarcely see, for her eyes were filled with tears.

Where were the words? Where were the stories?

It's just not a book of stories, without any words, she thought.

As the little girl paged through the wordless book,
she heard the wind blow and then a small whisper:

"Dear little girl, don't be disappointed.
You can imagine the words.
You can imagine the stories.
Start with a few simple words and imagine from there.
Remember: beginnings, middles, and ends of
stories can always be changed and imagined differently.
There are never any rules, rights, or wrongs in imagining—
imagining just is."

The whisper sounded so knowing and wise to the little girl
that she opened the book to the first page and began.

At first it felt difficult to imagine a story, so she looked harder at the picture. Are the bears best friends? she wondered. Maybe the Blue Bear is bringing honey as a gift. Bears love honey.

BLUE BEAR'S VISIT —now, that's a good title, she thought.
Then she began to tell herself a story: *Blue Bear arrived on the first day of spring.*
He promised . . .

The little girl studied the second picture. There's that little rabbit
again, she thought. I wonder what that man is saying to the magnificent ox? I know   . . .

THE SECRET *"Mr. Ox, you must please promise not to tell anyone, but we need your help. Last week . . ."*

The words began to come more and more easily to the little girl.
Then the words grew into sentences and the sentences became stories.

THE QUEST *Their hundred-mile journey began in a sturdy wooden boat. "Are we there yet?"
asked Rabbit. "In another two days and one night," replied Lion. "Oh, that's a very long time. I
forgot, please remind me again—where are we going?" asked Rabbit.*

TIGER'S PRAYER *All the creatures of the land near and far would be coming, and preparations were being made. The clown in the pointed hat would play music on his*

accordion. The wind horse would jump through hoops. Tea would be served exactly at noon, for
Tiger had something important to say . . .

A BIRTHDAY PARTY *As instructed, we arrived at exactly 3:33. One four-leaf
clover and a large pot of hot, steeping tea had been purposely placed near the entrance of the woods.
An owl perched in a tree to our left asked, "HOO WHO?" and we promptly answered with the*

secret password. Our job was to bring the birthday cake: vanilla with vanilla cream frosting and black raspberry filling with exactly six candles on top. Pan was very particular, and you could never quite know what to expect, but he insisted on throwing the surprise birthday party for . . .

THE MAGICAL CLOAK *One night, a mysterious man in an elaborate cloak sailed into our harbor. Quite quickly it became obvious to us that he was some kind of wizard or magician, for he could blow bubbles in the shapes of things. What was even more extraordinary was that the*

bubbles, once released, became real. Before long, enormous white whales filled our once calm harbor. Amazing as it was to see, we had to do something quickly to . . .

THE GOLDEN KEY *That very morning Owl told us he would pick us up at midnight. We must be on time and prepared for anything. He held the small golden key tightly in his beak as we*

flew into the indigo night sky. We were ready to face . . .

Word by word, hour after hour, the little girl imagined an entire story for each page.
And when the moon was full and bright, she grew sleepy and drifted off into a dream-
world woven out of the threads of the pictures and the stories she had imagined.

When she woke, the little girl felt grateful for the small knowing whisper. Already she missed her new friends the ox, the owl, and the tiger. She yearned to open the book once again, but the sun was up over the horizon and the birds were already fluttering about, chirping their morning songs. She did not want to be late for school, so she tidied herself, scooped up the book, and rushed out the door.

Along the path she met
a fox holding a
curiously round package.

"Excuse me, little girl,"
said the fox.
"I believe I have
the words to your book.
I saw them spill away,
and because I am
a very clever kind of fox,
I caught them in my net
just before they drifted
too far off."

"Oh, thank you,"
replied the little girl,
feeling a bit confused.

"Now, please,
before you leave,
could I bother you
for a small favor?"
asked the fox.

"Why, of course,"
answered the little girl.

The fox thanked the little girl and the little girl thanked the fox, and she gathered the book and the bundle of words and hurried down the path toward school once again.

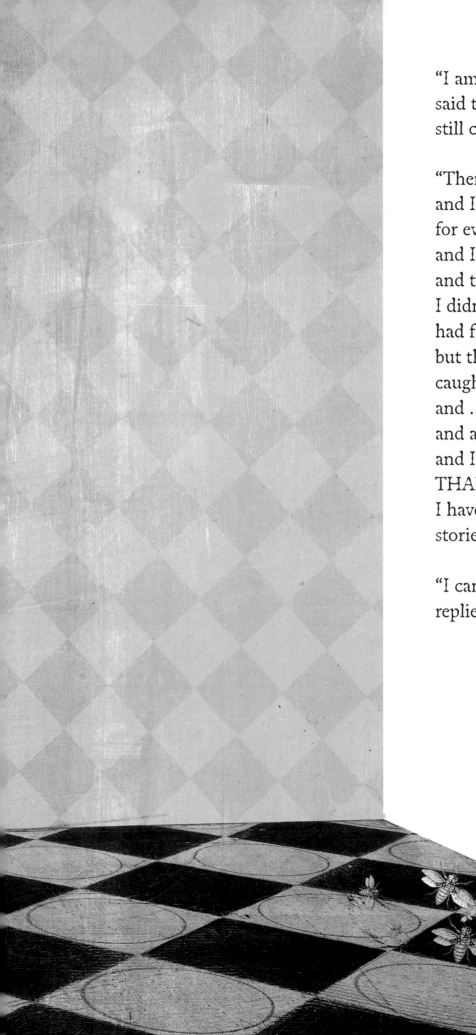

"I am so sorry I am late!"
said the little girl,
still catching her breath.

"There was a whisper,
and I imagined stories
for every picture . . .
and I overslept . . .
and the words,
I didn't know that they
had fallen away,
but the clever fox
caught them in his net
and . . . But I loved your book,
and and and
and I almost forgot,
THANK YOU!
I have so many
stories to tell you."

"I can't wait to hear,"
replied the teacher with a smile.

THE FOX AND THE GRAPES

A Famished Fox saw some clusters of ripe black grapes hanging from a vine. She resorted to all her tricks to get them, but wearied herself in vain, for she could not reach them. At last she turned away, beguiling herself of her disappointment and saying: "The Grapes are sour, and not ripe as I thought."

but this fox is
of the very clever kind,
so she imagined
her story differently

and the grapes tasted ever so sweet.

THE END